Blanket of Stars

Words by Jana Laiz & Sean Vernon
Music by Sean Vernon
Illustrated by Anastasiia Kuusk

Crow Flies Press
South Egremont, MA

CROW FLIES PRESS
PO BOX 614 SOUTH EGREMONT, MA 01258 (413)-281-7015
www.crowfliespress.com
publisher@crowfliespress.com

Blanket of Stars
ISBN ISBN:978-0-9814910-7-3
Copyright © 2018 Crow Flies Press
Illustrated by: Anastasiia Kuusk
Printed in the USA

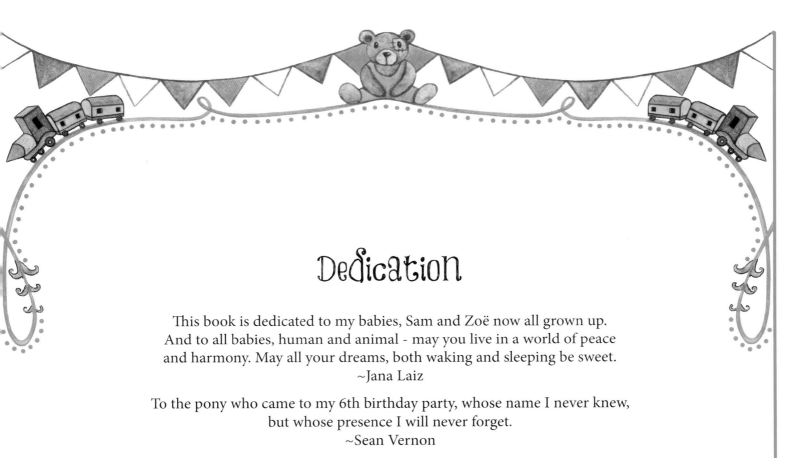

Dedication

This book is dedicated to my babies, Sam and Zoë now all grown up.
And to all babies, human and animal - may you live in a world of peace
and harmony. May all your dreams, both waking and sleeping be sweet.
~Jana Laiz

To the pony who came to my 6th birthday party, whose name I never knew,
but whose presence I will never forget.
~Sean Vernon

I dedicate my first book to my mom and dad who gave me my fabulous childhood,
and to my husband, with whom I am building a fabulous future.
~Anastasiia Kuusk

Night is falling on the hill
A busy world is getting still.
Crickets hum their soft refrain
While clouds drift in a silver chain.

Babies soon will be asleep,
in slumber peaceful warm and deep.
Bright stars twinkle in the sky
As mothers sing their lullaby…

Little Bird, it's time now
It's time for sleep.
Stop your flying and
come back to the nest.

It's so warm and cozy and
I'm waiting for you.
Come here and snuggle
under my wing and rest.

Little Bunny, come home
Come back to the den.
Stop your hopping and
lie down in the grass.

It's peaceful
on the hillside
underneath
the clouds.

Sleep in the starlight
and the night will pass.

A blanket of stars
Twinkles and covers you.

The wind sings a lullaby
'til the morning dew.

Little Fox, you're tired now
Get off your feet.
It's time to give up
wandering all around.

You've gone to the forest
You've walked along the road.
It's time to pause
and curl up on the ground.

The bees have all gone
to their hives to sleep.

The fish they are dozing
in the pond so deep.

In a yellow house
A young child's in bed.
The parents are both sleeping
Down the hall.

From the roof
You can hear the owl call.
He sees every movement
And he hears all.

But there's not a sound
From the horse's stall.

The only sound
is the swirling

of leaves as
they fall.

Bed in Summer
Robert Louis Stevenson (1850-1894)

In winter I get up at night
And dress by yellow candle-light.
In summer, quite the other way,
I have to go to bed by day.

I have to go to bed and see
The birds still hopping on the tree,
Or hear the grown-up people's feet
Still going past me in the street.

And does it not seem hard to you,
When all the sky is clear and blue,
And I should like so much to play,
To have to go to bed by day?

Who Has Seen the Wind?
Christina Rossetti (1830-1894)

Who has seen the wind?
Neither I nor you:
But when the leaves hang trembling,
The wind is passing through.

Who has seen the wind?
Neither you nor I:
But when the trees bow down their heads,
The wind is passing by.

Golden Slumbers
By Thomas Dekker (1572 – 1632)

Golden slumbers kiss your eyes,
Smiles awake you when you rise.
Sleep, pretty babies, do not cry,
And I will sing a lullaby:
Rock them, rock them, lullaby.

Care is heavy, therefore sleep you;
You are care, and care must keep you.
Sleep, pretty babies, do not cry,
And I will sing a lullaby:
Rock them, rock them, lullaby.

New Twinkle
By Sean Vernon

Far away, yes very far,
Past the moon, there lives a star
How it sparkles in the night,
it's very small but very bright

When there's no sun in the sky
The star is just a little spy
You never even know he's there
He's in the sky but who knows where

Now he's shining in the dark
Showing us his little spark
We couldn't see where we should go
Without the star's heavenly glow

You sit among the passing clouds
High above the earthly crowds
You won't ever go away
You won't wander, you won't stray

Jana has been a dreamer since she was a little girl. Nowadays, daydreaming and writing stories are her favorite things to do.

Sean is a writer, poet, singer, songwriter and musician. Sean has been writing songs since he was a kid and has no intention of stopping.

Anastasiia just draws. Drawing is her work and her hobby. She is drawing when she is happy, sad, inspired, annoyed, bored - always! But her drawings invariably remain cute and open-hearted. Just an artist, just a wife, just an adventurer.